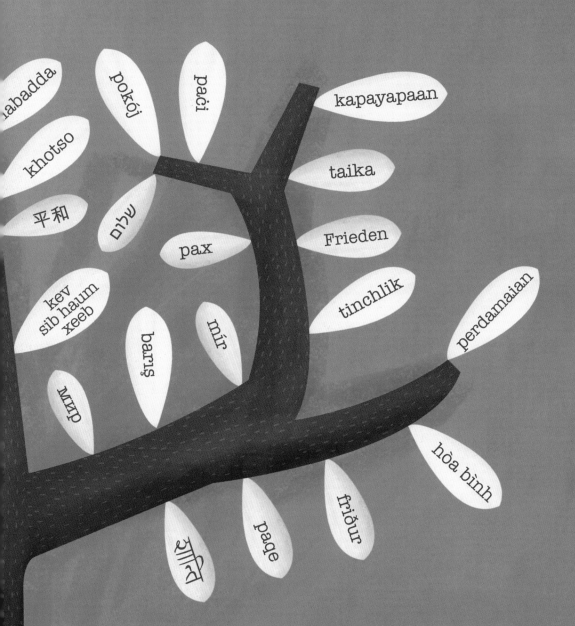

For Eugenie, Chris-Anne, and Ethan
and in loving memory of Christopher Moonie
– B. P. & M. P.

For all the children of the world
– E. M.

**Baptiste Paul** grew up in Saint Lucia. He loves sports, likes to roast his own coffee, and grills. His first book for NorthSouth was *The Field*, winner of the Sonia Lynn Sadler Award, a Junior Library Guild selection, and also appeared on the *Horn Book* Fanfare Best of 2018, the *School Library Journal* Best of 2018, and the CCBC 2018 Choices lists.

**Miranda Paul** has written more than a dozen children's books and has received several international awards. She is a founding member of the organization We Need Diverse Books and lives with her family in Wisconsin, USA.

**Estelí Meza** grew up surrounded by books and was already developing an early love for illustrations. In 2018 she was awarded the A la Orilla del Viento, Mexico's most important picture book award. Today Estelí lives in Mexico City, spends her time drawing, and always has a notepad and pen in hand.

# Peace

By Baptiste Paul & Miranda Paul

Illustrated by Estelí Meza

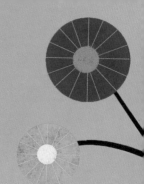

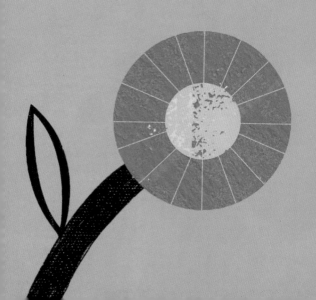

NorthSouth

Peace is a hello,
a smile,
a hug.

Peace can be bold
or quiet and snug.

Peace is pronouncing your friend's name correctly.

Peace means we talk
to each other directly.

Peace can begin with a laugh and a wave,
and grow into actions remarkably brave.

Peace comes from giving
far more than you take.
It's something we work toward,
it's something we make.

Peace is on purpose.
Peace is a choice.
Peace lets the smallest of us
have a voice.

Peace follows "I'm sorry,"
can let differences live.
It spreads and it strengthens
when hearts can forgive.

Peace is a pillow
that softens our sleep.

Peace pulls us through darkness
or up from the deep.

Peace is old like the stars
and new as a birth.

And if we embrace it
peace cradles the earth.

# Authors' Note

Sometimes we imagine world peace as a scenario in which all human beings get along. The truth, however, is that peace affects more than the humans who foster it. Peace can also impact animals and nature.

Recent studies have shown that when humans engage in violent conflicts, animals suffer—sometimes to the brink of extinction. In areas where humans aren't fighting, the opposite is generally true: animals benefit. Combined with conservation efforts, peace allows animals to thrive in areas once ravaged by war.

During our childhoods from 1977 to 1992, a beautiful country called Mozambique suffered through war. Many people lost their lives or were forced to flee their homes. The country also lost 90 percent of its wildlife. After the war, scientists counted only six lions and a hundred hippos left in one region. While that story is sad, the recovery afterward offers hope. Today, more than a hundred thousand wild animals roam Gorongosa National Park. Peacekeeping efforts have led to better health care, education, and economic development for the people who live there.

Some of the animals that appear in this book are ones you might find in Mozambique today, while others are cultural symbols of peace from nations around the world.

Peace can begin with a small step that you choose. A smile might spark a friendship. A friendship fosters empathy. Empathy leads to helpful actions. And helpful actions, over time, bring justice and peace.

With love,
Baptiste Paul & Miranda Paul

First published in the United States, Great Britain, Canada, Australia,
and New Zealand in 2021 by NorthSouth Books, Inc., an imprint of
NordSüd Verlag AG, CH-8050 Zürich, Switzerland.

Distributed in the United States by NorthSouth Books, Inc., New York 10016.
Library of Congress Cataloging-in-Publication Data is available.

ISBN: 978-0-7358-4449-0

Printed in Latvia, by Livonia Print, Riga
3 5 7 9 • 10 8 6 4 2
www.northsouth.com

Find out more:
www.baptistepaul.com
www.mirandapaul.com
www.estelimeza.com

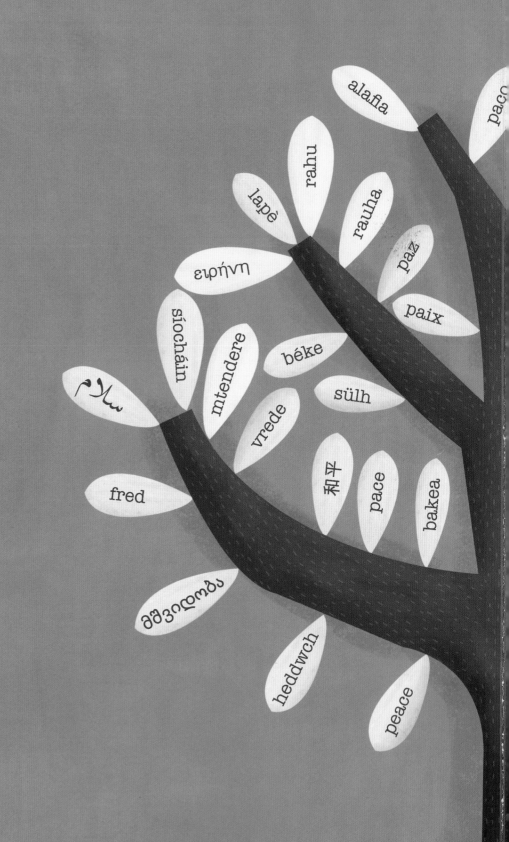